To Maya,
who will always be my Tummy Girl
—R. T.

To Helen the melon,
our very own snuggly girl
—S. W.

Henry Holt and Company, LLC
PUBLISHERS SINCE 1866
175 Fifth Avenue
New York, New York 10010

ISBN-13: 978-0-8050-7609-7

Designed by Patrick Collins
The artist used charcoal and pastels on 44-lb. paper to create
the illustrations, with color added digitally.
Printed in Mexico

TUMMY GIRL

Roseanne Thong

illustrated by Sam Williams

Henry Holt and Company ✦ New York

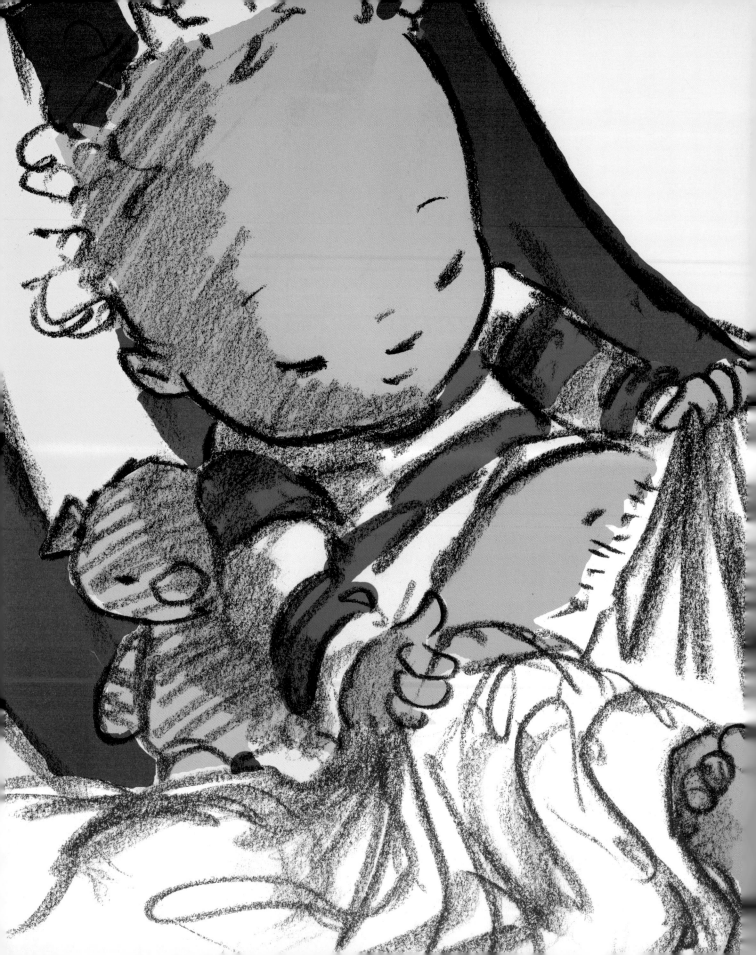

Once there was a tummy girl ...

. . . A full-of-warm-milk yummy girl,
A round-and-jiggly tummy girl,

Pink-as-a-piggly tummy girl,
Who loved to cuddle up and curl.

Once there was a bubble girl . . .

A getting-into-trouble girl,

A sudsy, wudsy bubble girl,

A washing-off-the-mudsy girl,

Who made the water swish and swirl.

Once there was a hiding girl . . .
A dash-from-mommy's side-ing girl,
A crawl-behind-the-curtain girl,
Beneath the chair, for CERTAIN girl,
Who scampered off just like a squirrel.

Once there was a waddling girl . . .
A teeter-totter toddling girl,
An "I can do it!" waddling girl,

A wrapped-in-cotton-swaddling girl,
Whose diapers started to unfurl.

Once there was a feeding girl . . .
While-mom-and-dad-were-reading girl,
A nice-big-spoonful-munching girl,
A drippy, milky, crunching girl,
Who stirred her breakfast with a swirl.

Once there was a running girl . . .
An in-the-rain-and-sunning girl,

A racing-through-the-thickets girl,
A chasing-bugs-and-crickets girl,
Who loved to dash and dart and whirl.

Once there was a swinging girl . . .
An "I'm so high, I'm singing" girl,
A try-to-reach-the-rooftops girl,
A love-to-feel-the-raindrops girl,
Whose long dark hair would spring and curl.

Once there was a dancing girl . . .
A stomping, bomping, prancing girl,
A two-step, three-step dancing girl,
A "you and me step" dancing girl,
Who loved to skip and jump and twirl.

Once there was a treetop girl . . .

As-far-as-she-could-see-top girl,

A lovely-place-for-snacking girl,

A nothing-here-is-lacking girl,

Who made the branches bend and curl.

Once there was a dressing girl . . .
Who-always-kept-us-guessing girl,
A fancy-hat-and-sundress girl,
A flashing, dashing, fun-dress girl,
Whose face was like a precious pearl.

Soon you'll be my older girl,
A taller-than-my-shoulder girl,
An "I can do it!" older girl,
A bigger, braver, bolder girl.
And though you'll grow up in a whirl . . .

...You'll always be my
Tummy Girl!